Bear Book

ISBN: 978-0-99076-0-8

Printed in the United States of America
Library of Congress catalog card number 2014952615

Visit us on the web!
www.bearbooksforkids.com

by Gloria Bowen

Illustrations by Kristina Lewis

For Jack, and for bear cubs everywhere

Scruffy bear, fluffy bear
Gobi bear grins

Grizzly cub plays with woodland friends

Brown bear, black bear,
big wet snout

Bears in the river catching trout

Panda bear, Atlas bear
quiet bear, loud

Bear on a mountain top,
bears in a cloud

Momma bear, Poppa bear
tiny bear, big

Some bears climb,
and some bears dig

Glacier bears romp on
the mountain all day

Sun bear, fun bear

Spectacled eyes

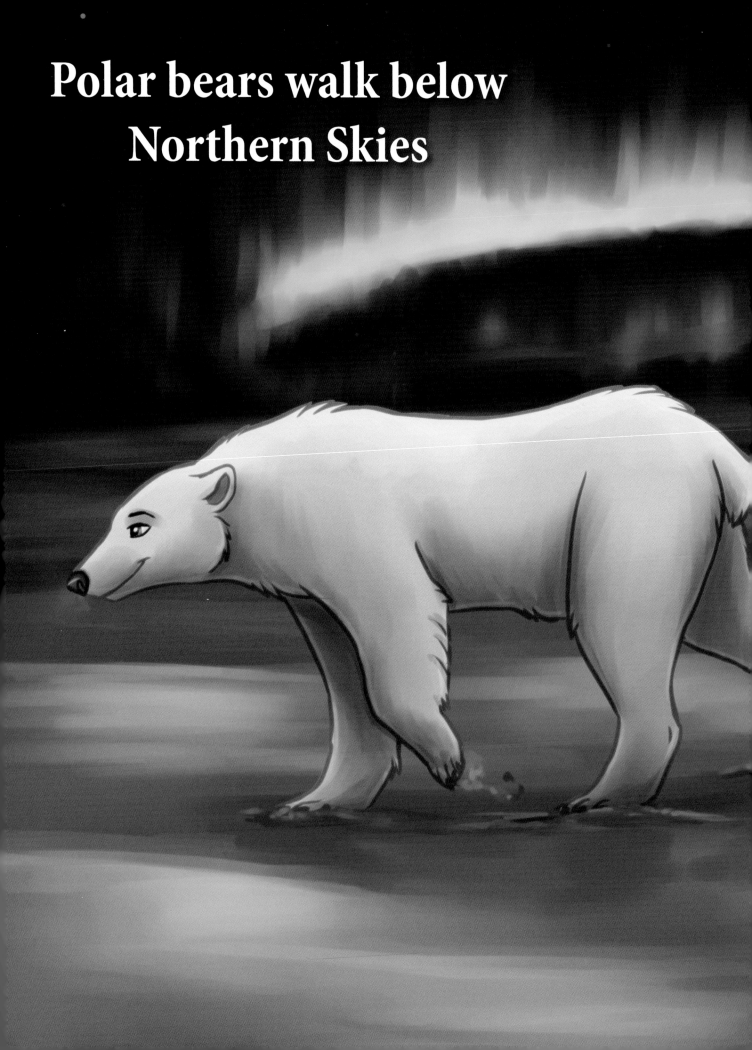

Polar bears walk below
Northern Skies

Here comes winter, starlings sing...

...time for bears to sleep 'til spring

Bear Books

www.bearbooksforkids.com